FCH Gr. 7

I Am Better Than You!

by

Robert
Lopshire

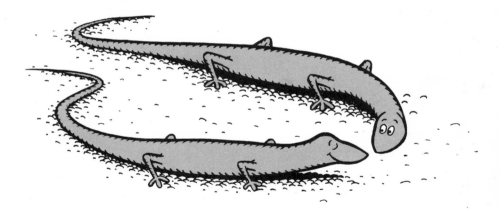

An I CAN READ Book®

Harper & Row, Publishers

I Can Read Book is a registered
trademark of Harper & Row, Publishers, Inc.

I AM BETTER THAN YOU!

Library of Congress Catalog Card Number: 68-24325
ISBN 0-06-023996-4
ISBN 0-06-023997-2 (lib. bdg.)

I Am Better Than You!

To Ineke, the world's foremost
authority on catching, feeding,
training, and keeping lizards.

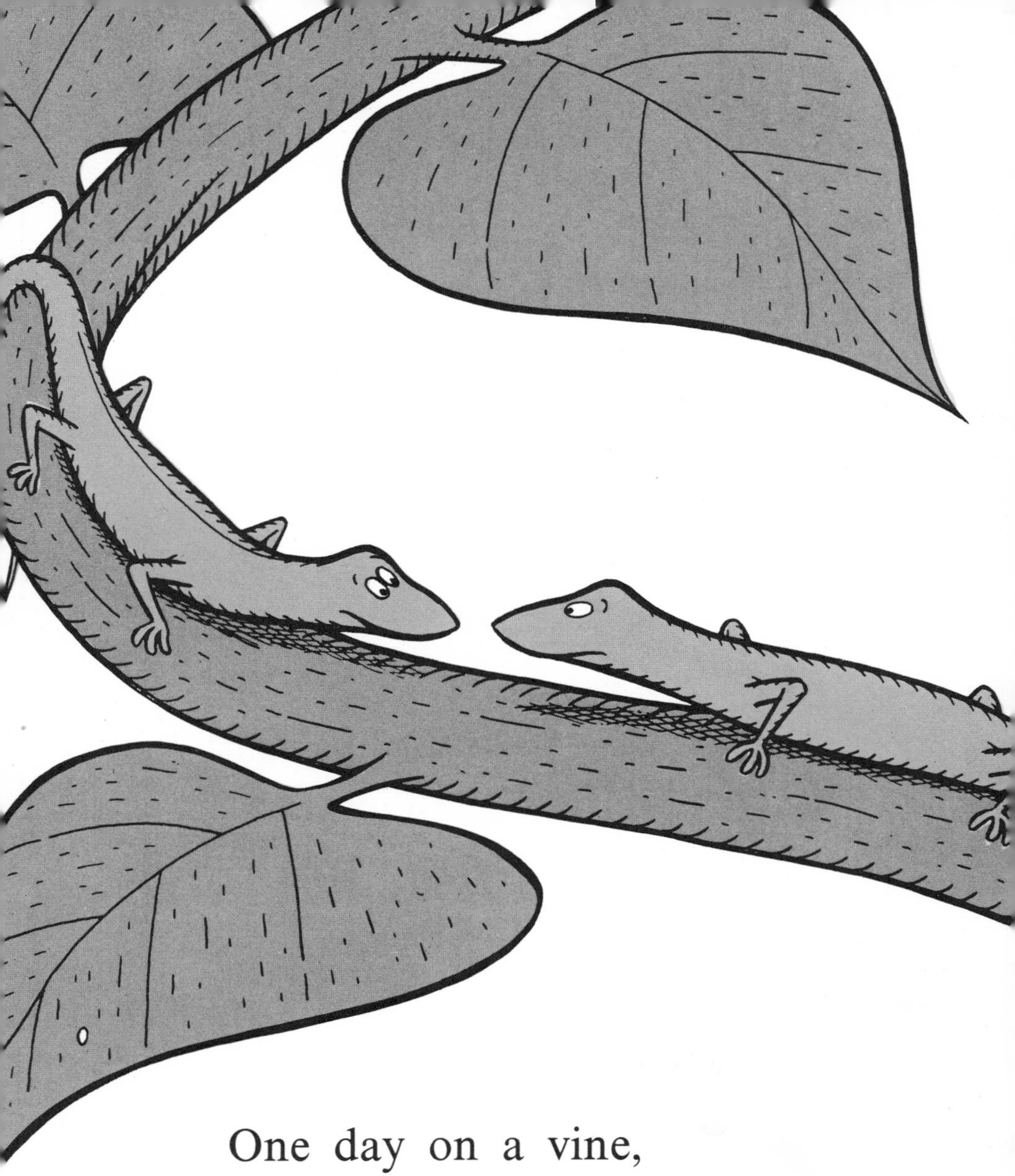

One day on a vine,

a lizard named Sam

met a lizard named Pete.

7

"Get out of my way!"

said Sam.

"Why?" asked Pete.

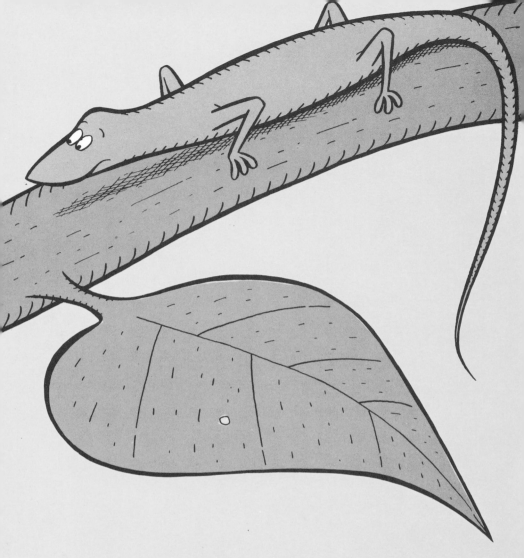

"Because," said Sam,

"I am the best lizard there is!"

"Why?" asked Pete.

"Why what?" asked Sam.

"Why are you

the best lizard there is?"

asked Pete.

"Because I am!" said Sam.

"But you look just like me,"

said Pete.

"No," said Sam.

"I am pretty. You are not."

"Oh," said Pete,

"I did not see that."

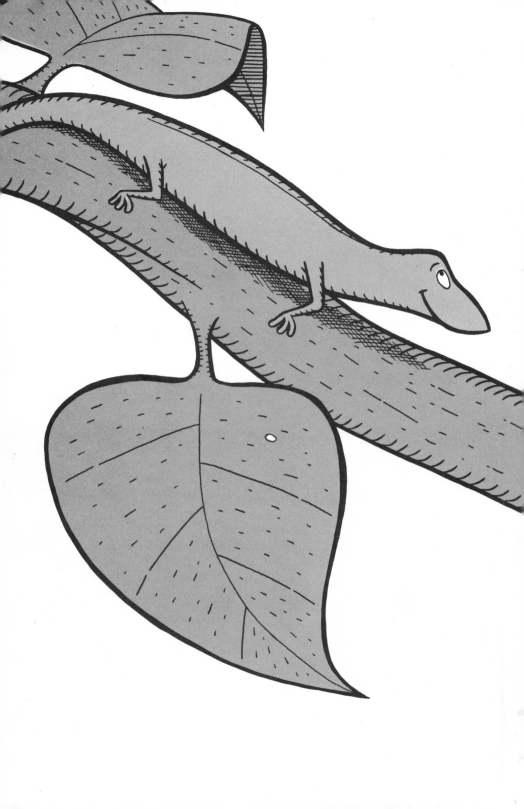

"I am much better than you,"
said Sam.
"I can do things
that you cannot do."
"Like what?" asked Pete.

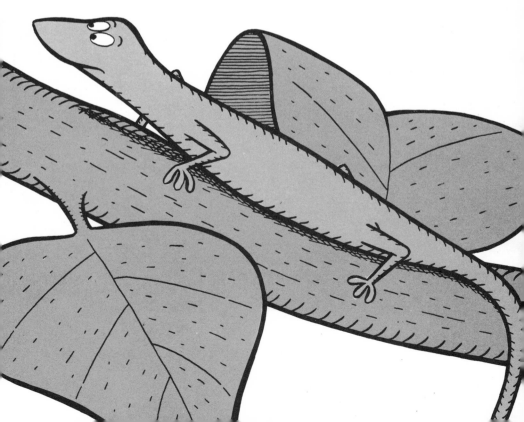

"I can catch a fly," said Sam.

Zap! Sam got a fly.

"I can do that," said Pete.

Zop! Pete got a fly too.

"Very funny," said Sam,

"but I am still better than you."

"Why?" asked Pete.

14

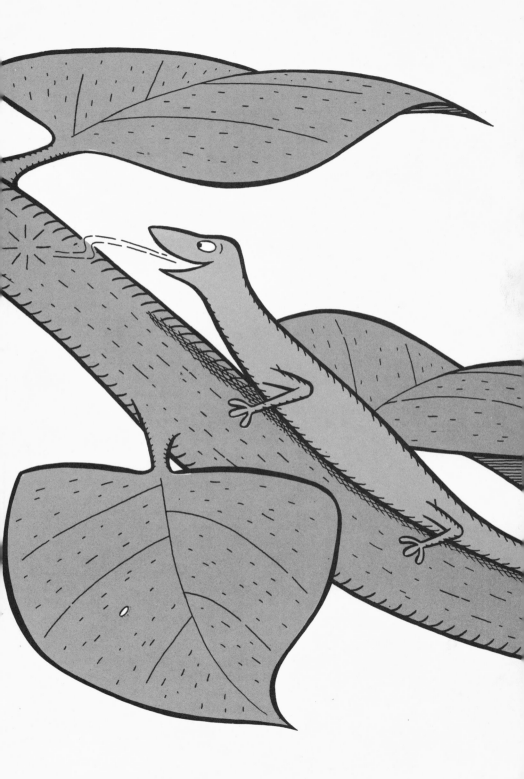

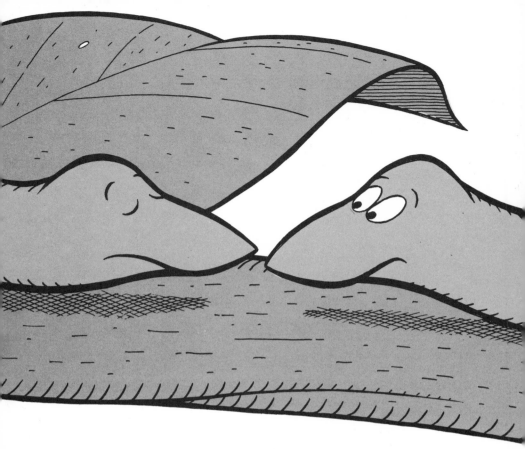

"You got a fly

who was sitting down,"

said Sam.

"I can get one

who is flying!"

16

Zup! Sam got a fly

who was flying.

"I know you cannot do that,"

he said.

Zop! Pete got a fly

who was flying.

"There," said Pete,

"I did what you did."

"You did not," said Sam.

"The fly you got

was looking the other way.

"I can get them when they look at me.

See, I will show you."

Zomp! Sam got a fly

who was looking at him.

"I think I can do that too," said Pete.

Zump! Pete got a fly

who was looking at him.

"Not bad," said Sam,

"but I am still the best

lizard there is.

I will show you why."

Zoop! "Did you see that?"

asked Sam.

"I got two flies with one shot!

I am the best lizard there is!"

"Wait," said Pete.

"Wait for what?" asked Sam.

"I would like to try

to get two flies with one shot,"

said Pete.

"Ha, ha," said Sam.

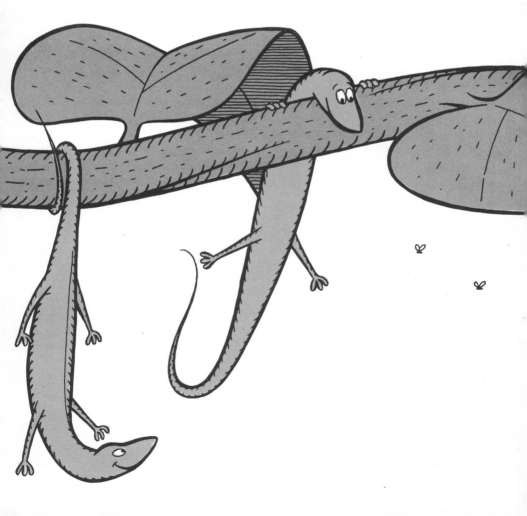

Zap! Pete got two flies.

"That was fun," said Pete.

"What will we do now?"

23

"You got two flies with one shot,"

said Sam,

"but I am still the best lizard.

I can get three with one shot!"

Zowp! Sam got three.

Zoop! Pete did it too.

"You are making me mad," said Sam.

"I said that I am the best

lizard there is," said Sam,

"and I am!

Watch me now.

I will get four flies with one shot."

Four flies came by.

Sam got ready.

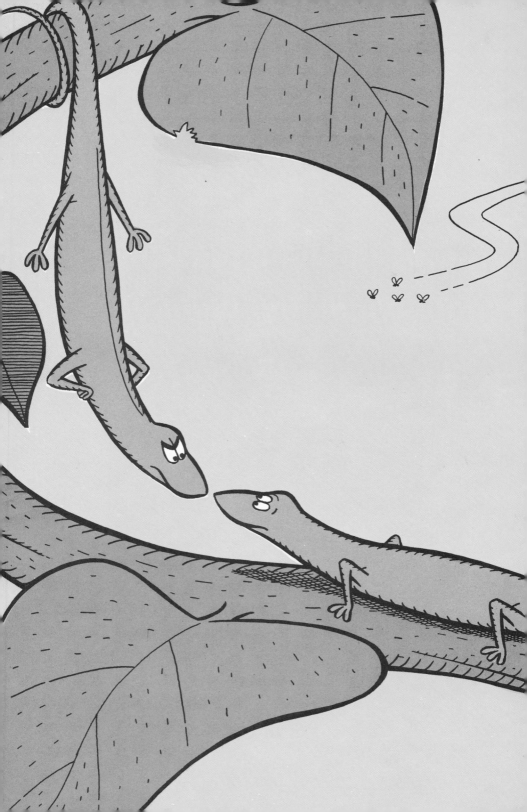

Zomp!

Sam missed.

The flies flew away.

Sam fell off the vine.

Pete laughed.

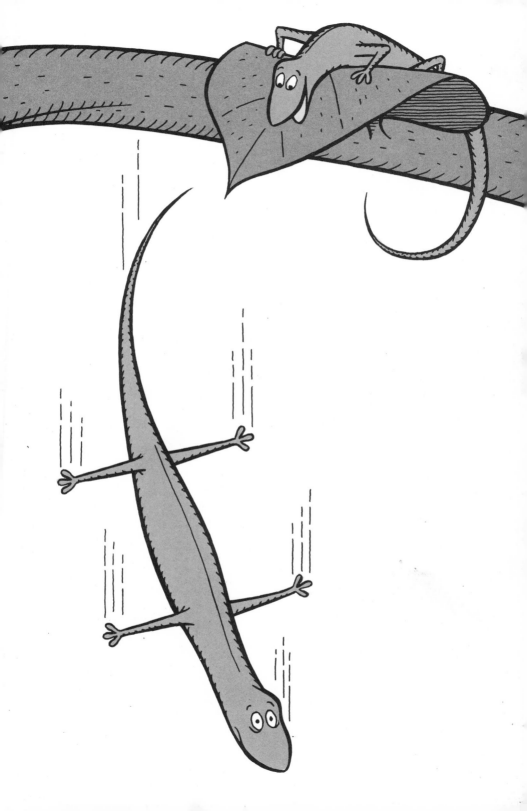

Pete went down to Sam.

"If you are the best

lizard there is,

why did you fall off

the vine?" asked Pete.

"I did not fall," said Sam.

"I came down

to do a new thing for you."

"Oh," said Pete.

"What are you going to do?"

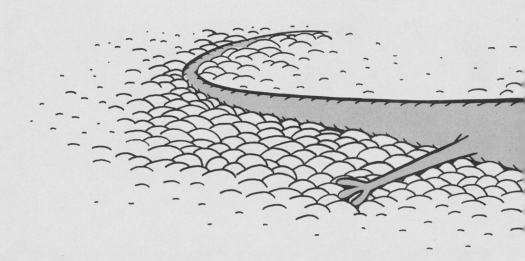

"I am the best lizard there is,"
said Sam.

"I will show you how fast
I can run."

Sam ran fast.

Pete ran beside him.

"This is fun!" said Pete.

"Be quiet," said Sam,

"or you will not see

how well I run!"

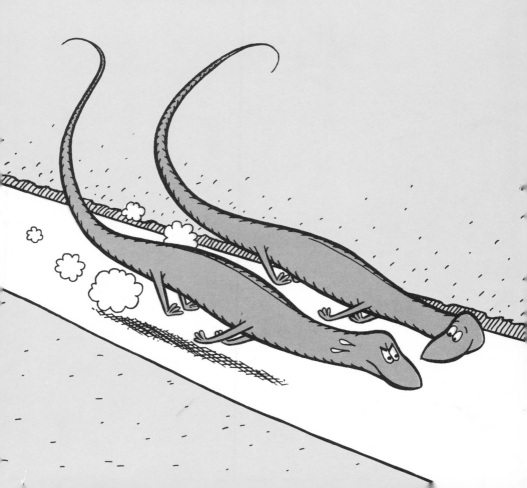

Sam ran into a tree.

BANG!

34

"Ooh!" said Pete.

"You did not see the tree!"

"I did see the tree," said Sam.

"I came here to show you

how good I am!

I will show you a thing

that you have not seen!"

"What is that?" asked Pete.

"I can make myself
turn a new color!"
said Sam.
"I can be the color
of what I sit on!
See! Now I am brown!
Now you know
that I am the best
lizard there is!"
"Why?" asked Pete.

"I am the best lizard there is,"
said Sam,
"because I made myself
turn brown!"
"You are a nice color of brown,"
said Pete,
"but I can do that too. See?"
"I see," said Sam,
"but your brown
is not as good as my brown."

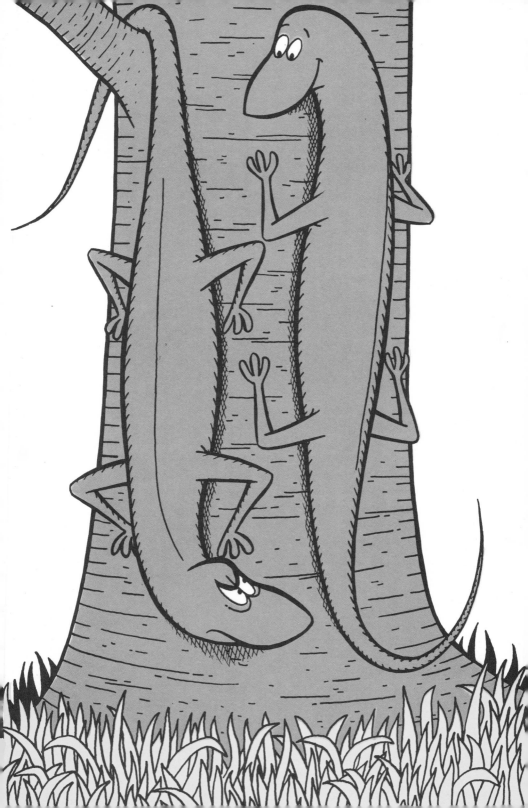

"You can be brown," said Sam,

"but I can be green!

See? I am the same color

as this leaf!

I am better than you.

I am the best lizard there is!"

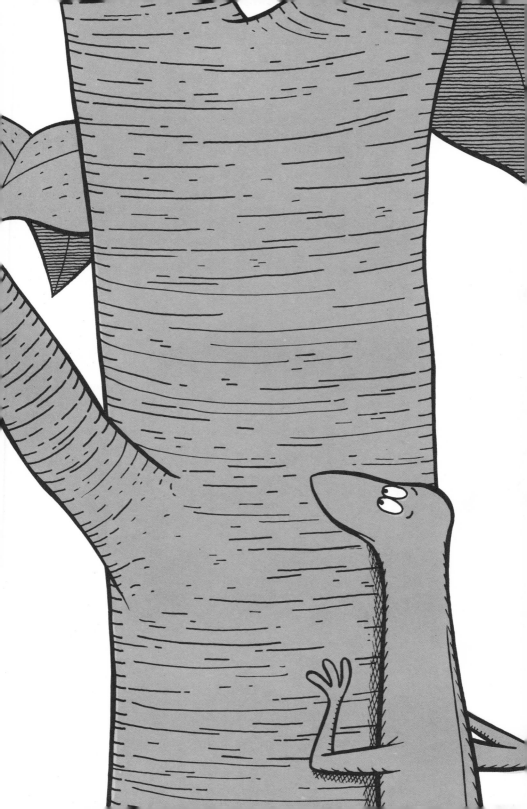

"I can do that," said Pete.

"Look at me.

I am the same green as you."

"No, you are not!" said Sam.
"I am a much better green
than you."

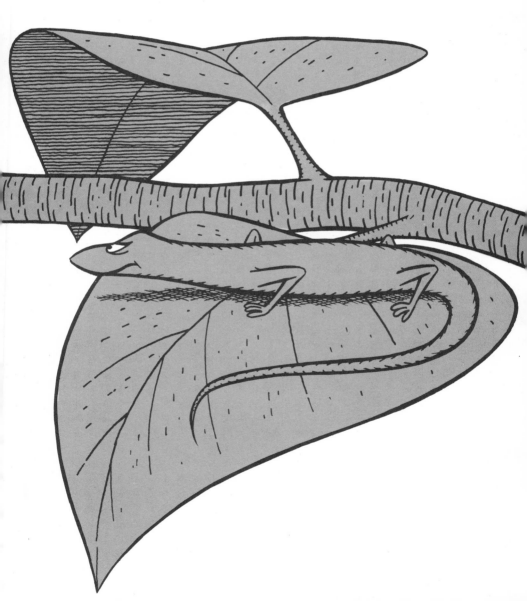

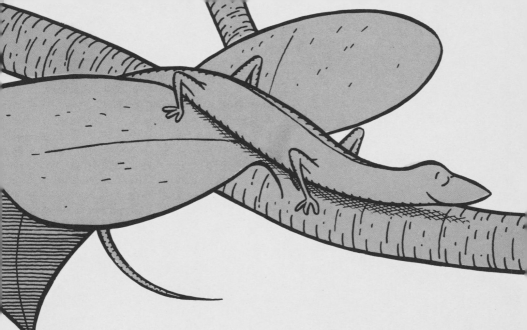

"You can be brown.

You can be green,"

said Sam.

"But I can be brown and green

at the same time!

So I am the best lizard

there is!"

"I have not done that before,"

said Pete.

"It looks like fun!

I will try it!"

"Ha, ha," said Sam,

"I know you cannot do it.

No one is as good as I am!"

Pete made himself

brown and green.

"Say! I can do it too!"

he said.

"*Hmph!*" said Sam.

"I am still better than you.

I will show you!"

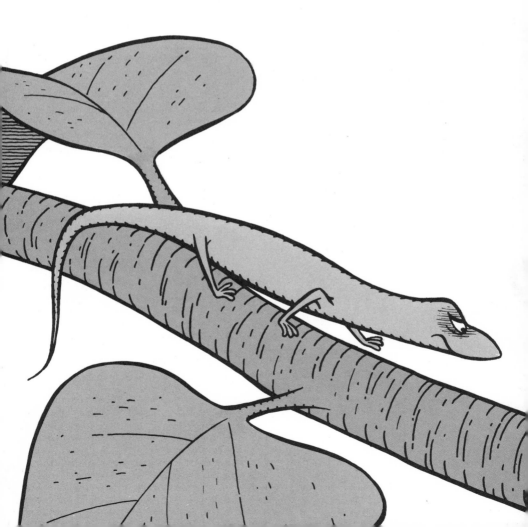

"There is some paper over there,"
said Sam.

"It has many colors on it.

I will make myself

turn all those colors!"

"I do not think

I can do that," said Pete.

"Well I can," said Sam,

"because I am the best

lizard there is!"

Sam went to the paper.

He got on it and sat down.

"Watch this!" he said.

"You are brown all over,"

said Pete.

"Be quiet!" said Sam.

"I am not ready yet.

I will make myself

all these colors.

Just watch me!"

Pete sat down to watch.

"I think I did it," said Sam.

"You are still brown," said Pete.

"Be quiet!" said Sam.

"I cannot do it

if you are not quiet!"

"I am sorry," said Pete.

"You should be," said Sam.

"It is hard work

being the best lizard there is."

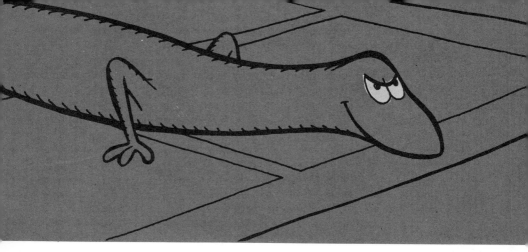

Night came.

Sam was still on the paper.

Pete was still watching.

"Look at me," said Sam.

"Now I am all the colors

that are on this paper."

"I am looking," said Pete,

"but I cannot see

what color you are.

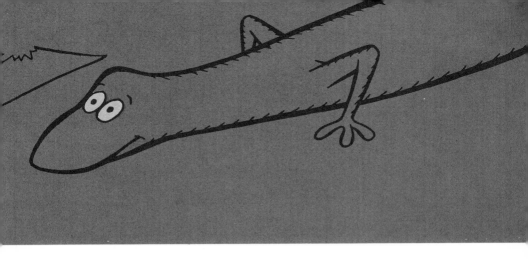

"I cannot even see you.

It is too dark."

"Too bad," said Sam.

"I am very pretty this way!"

"I wish I could see you," said Pete.

"Me too," said Sam.

"Then you would know

that I am the best lizard

there is!"

The sun came up.

"Now you can see me," said Sam.

"See how pretty I am?"

"I see you," said Pete,

"and I see that you are still brown.

You did not make yourself

all the colors on that paper.

You are not

the best lizard there is.

But you are best at one thing."

"What is that?" asked Sam.

"You are best at having
a big mouth," said Pete.
"I did each thing that you did,
but I did not get on that paper.
I know that lizards like us
can only be brown or green.
Any lizard knows that.
If you were the best lizard
there is,
you would know it too."

"Where are you going?" asked Sam.

"I am going back
to catch flies," said Pete.
"That is what lizards are best at,
so that is what I will do."

"May I come with you?"

asked Sam.

"Yes," said Pete,

"if you will be quiet."

"I will," said Sam.

"I will be very quiet."